WOLF
VS
ORB

Also by Alexandria Blaelock

FICTION
That Love Nonsense
Taipan vs Brown
The Ghost and Ms Cox
Friends Like That
Weaving the Wildwood
Wolf vs Orb

SHORT STORY COLLECTIONS
Lovelorn, Lovestruck and Love at First Sight
Histories of Hayward Hall
Common or Garden Variety Heroes
Case Files of the Wilkinson National Detective Agency
Unavoidable Fates
Christmas Travesties
Five Faces of Felicia Clarke
Little Place Called Home
Security Directorate Dossiers volume 1
Security Directorate Dossiers volume 2

MS BLAELOCK'S BOOKS
Stress Free Dinner Parties
Signature Wardrobe Planning
Holistic Personal Finance
Minimally Viable Housekeeping
Planning a Life Worth Living

PICTURE BOOKS
Australia Felix

SELECTED SHORT STORIES

Alma's Grace	Life in the Security Directorate
Balancing the Book	Needy Bitch
Bygone Boyfriend	Onslaught at New Mir
Christmas Bonanza	Payton's Run
Dwennon's Despair	Secret Singer
Fate in Your Hands	Shining Star
Honeymoon Disaster	Ship in a Bottle
Kiss of Death	The Shadow Thieves
Lady of the Looking Glass	The Palace Hotel

WOLF
VS
ORB

A GEORGIA GARSIDE
PRIVATE DETECTIVE NOVELLA

ALEXANDRIA BLAELOCK

BlueMere Books
MELBOURNE, AUSTRALIA

For permission requests, please contact
enquiries@bluemerebooks.com.

Ordering Information:
Discounts are available on quantity purchases. For details, contact
orders@bluemerebooks.com.

Wolf vs Orb/Alexandria Blaelock
hardback ISBN: 978-1-923083-16-5
paperback ISBN: 978-1-923083-17-2
digital ISBN: 978-1-923083-18-9

Book Layout © BookDesignTemplates.com
Cover Art © Marie Žáková/Depositphotos

In Memory of Binky

Speak softly and carry a big stick; you will go far.

– THEODORE ROOSEVELT

1

I ran down Abbot Street as if my life depended on it.

Which it kind of did.

Not because I was running for my life, though I kind of was.

And not because there was another bomb, or I was trying to avoid a car crash, or a tram was going to leave without me if I didn't get on it in a nanosecond.

Nor a crazed, escaped prisoner, demon, or slavering dog attempting to bite me.

Quite simply, I ran because I was afraid.

Afraid of being stabbed.

Again.

I mean, I *knew* the majority of people go about their lives without being confronted by knife-wielding maniacs.

And only a very small proportion of people actually grow up to become knife-wielding maniacs.

And I, Georgia Garside, licensed private investigator and bodyguard, had somehow got through thirty-odd years of not meeting, let alone being threatened, or having a knife inserted into my body by a knife-wielding maniac.

But still, when it happened, I wasn't prepared.

And while I'd been surprised, the woman hadn't leapt out of nowhere with a knife, but had knifed me in the ribs *immediately* after I'd got a fucking gun off her.

Like one of those goddamned movie villains that just won't bloody die.

Even after you've shot them, blown them up, and driven over them with a sky-blue B-double truck and trailer.

Reversing just to make sure.

Twice!

She'd gone to prison for twenty-five years, with a non-parole period of eighteen.

But even after months spent convalescing, I wasn't convinced I'd recovered my full fitness or capacity post-incident.

I was convinced I was carrying a potentially lethal instant of hesitation between seeing and reacting.

The kind of hesitation that knife, machete or sword-wielding maniacs can, and do, take advantage of.

The kind that gets you killed.

A bit of a deficiency when it comes to protecting clients.

And, of course, myself.

So, I'd woken in my small rooftop apartment, thrown on some black leggings and a red tank top.

Because if red cars go faster, so too must red tank top-wearing runners.

Ran down the fire escape stairs, and towards the park to take a lap or two around its forested section.

To rebuild my fitness, and practise my observational skills.

Leaving my music player in my apartment, because I was frightened and needed to hear what was going on around me.

Rather than the latest episode of the cold case podcast I used to love.

So, after hearing an elderly lady squawk as a knife-wielding bag snatcher relieved her of her handbag.

Viciously wrenching it off her shoulder.

I changed course and ran after said knife-wielding bag snatcher.

Mainly because I was running anyway.

And it'd been too much of an effort to slow down to see if the elderly, recently handbag-deprived lady needed a different kind of assistance.

Perhaps the kind you get from ambulance officers.

Anyhow, there is always a dearth of people to do the actual running.

Most people witnessing traumatic acts generally freeze and don't do anything to help.

They're too afraid of getting hurt themselves or worse, looking like an idiot.

They need someone to take charge.

So, I'd changed course, slowing down a little as I did.

Grabbing some guy wearing a pin-stripe suit by the shoulder, shouting in his face, "call an ambulance," shaking his arm, "I'm going for the bag."

I sped up as I ran past him.

Given it was a warm, cloudless, yet not too hot day, it was almost the perfect conditions for running.

Enough to cover my back with a slight layer of sweat, clammy against my allegedly water-wicking tank top.

Though it's also possible I was a bit nervous.

Ruthlessly forcing myself out of my comfort zone.

As I chased down the bag snatcher, settling into a comfortable lope, dodging around dawdling pedestrians, rubberneckers, and shop displays mounted on the sidewalk.

The wide, recently poured, and still mostly white concrete sidewalk radiated its sun-warmed heat up at me from the ground.

The reflections from the sheet glass windowed store frontages were so bright I couldn't see what was inside them.

Though I did notice the extra layer of waist-height warm air pockets I was running through.

The smell of hot concrete joined the airborne odours of tram stop rubbish bins.

As I ran, I pondered whether the aromas of gently rotting food might have worse health implications than had previously been identified.

Nearing the street's single remaining street tree, a poor, stunted specimen, drooping in the heat, I heard a piteous meow.

Glancing up into the branches I saw the solution to an as yet unsolved mystery on my books; a missing white and orange tabby cat named Binky.

One of a spate of missing cats. All of them female.

God knew how Binky had gotten so far away from home.

Probably via another thief looking for a different kind of score.

Given the missing cats were all female, perhaps hoping to breed her.

Abandoning her when the de-sexing tattoo in her ear was discovered.

That they had dumped Binky so far away from her home was telling.

Most likely operating somewhere near where Binky lived.

Running by the tree, I wondered whether the blood-purifying benefits of building up a sweat were dissipated by lung-clogging inhalations of car exhaust.

Regardless of whether unleaded petrol was generally "healthier" than leaded.

Happily, being a lot fitter than the average knife-wielding bag snatcher, I was by then, close enough to reach out and grab its hoodie.

Bringing the apparently male teenaged thief to an abrupt, choking stop.

Can't quite believe he didn't dump the bag, but I suppose he was desperate to get away and forgot he was running away with a black patent Kelly-style bag hanging off his shoulder.

Looked good on him too.

Recovering, he wrenched himself out of my grasp and pulled out his knife again.

Dancing around, knife in his right hand, slashing it to the left and then the right.

Holding it as if he was trying to carve a joint of meat.

Managed not to roll my eyes.

Waited until he stopped dancing from side to side and committed to stepping forward to stab me.

I grinned.

He checked for a fraction of a second, and that was enough.

Brought my hands together, simultaneously slapping his wrist with my right, and the back of his hand with my left.

The knife went flying.

Wrenched his arm to my left forcing his shoulder down.

As his hand rolled, I clasped it in both of mine.

Applied my thumb to the joint of his middle finger and forced him to his knees.

Didn't even have to think about it.

A small round of applause from a crowd that had gathered while I was focused on him.

See?

People don't want to commit to taking action.

They tell themselves they'll help as soon as the situation gets out of control, and yet they're frozen in place.

Takes a nut job like me to do something.

But I was delighted with the outcome, disarming him on autopilot was immensely gratifying.

This feat made it crystal clear that I *could* rely on my body to take over the physical work while my brain took care of strategy.

Such as it was.

Not my crystal, obviously, because:

a) my crystal is not actually crystal, and

b) if it was actually crystal, it would be as smeared as fuck; covered in soap scum and fingerprints.

But definitely as clear as Mother's crystal, which is actually crystal, and utterly spotless.

It was a huge relief.

I just can't tell you.

Though I expect by now you're wishing I'd move on.

After disarming the boy, I accepted the knife from a witness who'd used her handkerchief to pick it up off the street.

Pushed the boy, by the arm I held behind his back, back to his elderly victim, and forced him to apologise.

Properly.

The elderly victim tried to reward me with a gold coin, which was no doubt a substantial sum of money to her, the state of the pension system being what it is, but as the self-proclaimed Robin Hood of private investigators, I gracefully declined.

Honour satisfied, fit and functional self three-quarters redeemed, I left him to the police officer who'd belatedly arrived on scene.

2

I returned to Binky, for whom I could invoice for slightly more than a gold coin.

I was fully prepared to climb the tree.

Or perhaps, given the stunted growth, just pull a branch low enough to scoop the cat off it.

"It's all right Binky," I said, "you're safe now."

The cat dropped from the branch, landing lightly in my outstretched arms.

Job well done if I do say so myself.

Poor Binky was a pampered pussy, bewildered and somewhat bedraggled after a few days on the street.

Nothing in common with the lean, mean and street smart big black cat, known as BBK, who'd adopted me before my office was blown up.

Now living a less exciting, half-indoor life at Gran's place.

Binky settled herself on a forearm, leaning against my chest, and snuggled into my neck with a deafening purr.

We walked back to my new office/apartment in Gran's three-story building.

Aside from being clean, in so far as buildings go, the new one was exactly the same as the old one that'd been blown to bits.

Perhaps explaining how Gran had got it through planning and constructed in record time.

I don't know why Gran decided to rebuild exactly the same building. Nor do I, given the fact it's a retro seventies monstrosity, know where she got the materials from.

The roughly textured dark brown bricks I kind of get, but the orange tiles? Must all be second-hand, because where else did the lichen come from?

Though I concede it could've been painted on.

But it still begs the question, why?

The building looks like a ziggurat, a kind of squared-off pyramid, the floor size decreasing from ground to second to third to rooftop.

Each of the stories has a kind of balcony, clad in orange tile, such that the building appears to be an ancient Aztec construction of brown and orange stripes.

Aside from the obvious thing of Aztecs not being big brick users.

Or Australian.

The fire escape snakes up a wall alongside the alley, screened by a lace work of bricks that also provides an outside area for the usual small colony of smokers.

There's something about the stripes and the third floor that means you can't see the rooftop apartment from the ground.

The original building felt to me like the builders ran out of money and couldn't afford to give it the white render to call it Spanish colonial style.

The new one does too.

Though to be honest, I think Gran might have fudged the deceptively spacious apartment I live in on the roof - I'm sure it wasn't always that big.

Perhaps the elevators were fudged too - one of them goes non-stop from the ground to the roof.

As far as I could tell, the previous landlord kept his junk corralled in something more like a small room on the rooftop. Along with his not quite lawful or legal garden.

If you know what I mean.

Now there is a luxurious garden with some decking and a pergola shading a table and four chairs, a large, shallowish blue ceramic bowl of water with a small fountain and planter boxes with fruit, vegetables and ornamentals.

One of the corners catches the sun all day and that's where the washing line went.

Disguised as part of my fitness trail come outdoor gym come *parcours* circuit with a pull-up bar, balance beams, parallel dip bars, stepping posts, and a pole climb.

In combination with the pots, the obstacles, and my weights, I can get a good upper *and* lower body workout, as well as balance and coordination, all without leaving home.

And the *pièce de résistance*, a green and white striped hammock I hung between the pull-up bar and the washing line.

Yes, I know. Gran took care of me very well.

Each of the floors, including the roof, has a foyer where you can wait for the elevator or access the fire escape stairs. The foyers are locked, isolating the various offices, so you have to be buzzed through.

The roof door is supposed to be automatically locked. You're not supposed to be able to get up without buzzing me to grant you access to the apartment.

But half the time I forget to lock it.

It's not like the door opens directly into the apartment anyway.

I think Gran thought I'd feel more secure that way, and I do, but it might've been better to have a small office in the building as well.

Or somewhere else entirely.

But I don't make enough money to afford two rents, and even assuming Gran would permit me to pay just one, Mother wouldn't allow it.

As it was, I usually took the stairs, because they were faster than the elevator.

Trying as best I could to not actually look at the building until I was inside it.

But cats not being the kind of creatures that take kindly to be bounced around, I decided to take the elevator.

The apartment itself has a large (for an apartment) open-plan kitchen, dining, and lounge room. Two bedrooms (one I use for work), and a combined bathroom laundry between the bedrooms.

I've only been there a few weeks, so the white paint is still blindingly white when you open the curtains.

Which are also white, though annoyingly, not the exact same white. Thankfully they're sun-blocking otherwise I'd be awake way too early every day.

The furniture is wooden, simple and elegant, and must have cost a fortune.

Gran knows I can barely find my mouth to eat or drink without spilling or dropping it.

So, there are dark carpets on the floor, and a couch with a brightly coloured, wildly abstract floral pattern that is such utter hell when I'm hung over, I've covered it with a clashing blue plaid blanket.

Which is slightly better but also hell when I'm hung over.

Not being a cat owner, I don't have any cat food. But I do have snack-sized tins of tuna for when I can't be bothered with the complexities of feeding myself, so I crossed my fingers and rummaged around for a tin of tuna to feed Binky.

She hoed into it, meowing "nyum, nyum, nyum," until she'd eaten it all.

I deduced she hadn't eaten for a couple of days.

Then took a drink of water from the fountain, and plopped herself in a sunbeam to give herself a bath.

I did likewise.

And after a proper shower, in the bathroom, changed into my favourite black jeans and t-shirt with fresh red sneakers.

Called Binky's owner, "I've got your cat, when would you like me to drop her around?"

"Ah. Oh. Well... It's not exactly convenient right now."

I clenched my lips, trying not to let any of the bad thoughts I was having leak out through them, "I see."

"We're having some work done around the house you see? And it might be better for Binky not to be here while we're doing it."

Why oh why?

Why would you hire a private detective to find your cat, and then get "some work done around the house?"

I ask you again, why?

Do you have no confidence the cat will ever be recovered?

"Look, we'll pay you the finder's fee, that's five hundred bucks. And the cattery charges thirty bucks a night, so say two weeks, and that's four hundred and twenty, so let's round it up to a grand and we'll come get her then?"

I counted to ten and double-checked the calculations.

"I've got your account details, so... I'll... transfer it now..."

My phone pinged with a payment notification for one thousand dollars.

I sighed.

"Fine, but only two weeks. Don't make me remind you to come get her."

"Oh, that's great, thanks so much, we owe you big time!"

And she hung up before I could change my mind.

Wise move on her part.

Two weeks didn't sound enough.

You know what they say, renovations always take twice as long and three times as much money.

"What a fucking shit show," I said out loud, to no one in particular.

"Un-fucking-believable."

And then I turned around to see Binky, paused, in the act of leaning her body around to groom her back leg, stuck up high in the air.

She looked as dubious as I felt.

It was probably the renovations that scared her off, not that she'd been catnapped as the owners had told me.

"What do you reckon?" I asked her, "was it the renovations?" She stood up and walked away, tail held high, the tip twitching back and forth insolently.

About the same as me then.

So I sighed, dragged my laptop out, typed up an invoice, attached a receipt, and emailed it off.

But at least I got paid.

I *love* instant bank transfers.

Plus, there's something incredibly satisfying about collecting all your papers together into a file and stamping it CLOSED in bright red ink.

Filing it away, on a shelf, next to all your other closed cases.

Though given business was slow picking up after the explosion...

There weren't that many files.

I'd just got my website up and running again.

But thought I really ought to put up cards in the local supermarkets or maybe some flyers to put in local letter-boxes.

Then sighed and added a note to my calendar to remind me to get back in touch with Binky's people after a week and a half.

So that was all that, *and* I got my mojo back.

Fighting fit!

All in all, a very good morning if I do say so myself.

3

Made a quick instant coffee, topped a couple of crispbread with a slice of ham, cheese and a fresh tomato from the garden via my fruit bowl. Sprinkled it with a tonne of freshly ground black pepper.

Took it out under the pergola to read the newspaper.

Perused the "Help Wanted" and "Missing" notices, because you never know.

Not that many people actually put ads in the paper these days. Most of it goes on social media.

And I can't be bothered scrolling through social media.

Unless I'm working on a case and need a bit of intel.

It used to be the paper might take you half a day to read, but now it's not even enough to drink a large cup of coffee, let alone eat an open sandwich.

Boredom forced me to do a little light cleaning and hang out a load of washing.

Then I walked around the roof a bit, did a little half-hearted training.

Flung myself into the hammock and replayed disarming the teenager to see if there was anything I could do better next time.

Though to be honest, it seems like replaying the past to see what I can learn from it is becoming too much of a habit.

Watered the plants, pulled off a few dead leaves and flowers, pulled up a few weeds attempting to sprout.

Just when I was about bored enough to throw myself off the building, I heard a female voice, "um hello? Are you Georgia Garside?"

I turned and smiled noncommittally, nodding at the tall, thin, middle-aged woman.

Shoulders hunched, hands clasped firmly in front of her, jaw lightly clenched.

With her long face, beaky nose, and deep red hair, she looked vaguely familiar.

Had I seen her around?

Yet, with a face that striking, it was unlikely you'd confuse her with anyone else.

She unclasped and re-clasped her hands in front of her as she wrung them a little.

"I've come about my daughter."

"Would you like to take a seat?" I gestured at the pergola, "some coffee perhaps?"

Her shoulders dropped as she nodded and scuttled across the roof to the pergola.

Something about the way her body stayed still, while her legs moved in a short, angular, outward movement was strange and unsettling.

Like a huntsman spider.

Walking across the roof while you're lying on your bed underneath it.

Out of sight, in the kitchen, I shuddered.

Made a fresh pot of drip filter coffee, leaving her to enjoy the view.

Or the newspaper.

Or whatever.

When the coffee was done, I put it on a slightly rusty rose patterned tray with a small jug of milk, bowl of sugar, and a couple of spoons and mugs.

Flower mug for her, chipped cartoon superhero for me.

Emptied a packet of plain biscuits in a heap on a plate.

Good for gnawing.

Or dunking.

I don't know why sweet biscuits always loosen tongues.

Especially the dunking ones.

Added a new daybook for a new investigation and a pen.

Then took the tray outside.

"Milk? Sugar?" I asked sliding the tray onto the table.

"Milk and one sugar please."

As almost everyone prefers.

Didn't say anything as I decanted the coffee and pushed the mug towards her, then the biscuits.

Poured the other mug for me, set my daybook and pen on the table, and put the tray aside.

She sipped, cupping the mug in both hands, and made an appreciative noise.

I do make a good coffee if I say so myself. I get the grounds from a speciality grinder nearby.

While I waited for her to say something, I studied her clothing, loose black track pants, white t-shirt, black zip-up fleece jacket. Loose enough to be men's clothing.

So annoying.

Half the recent fashions for women are loose clothing.

Which really just lets the shops sell you cut-down men's clothes - all the buttons and zips on the wrong fucking side.

Bloody annoying.

One thing I hate about online shopping - they sell you all the rubbish and make it hard to send it back for refunds when it turns out you've been conned.

In my opinion, that's way more worthy of a conspiracy theory than enslaved kids tucked away in the drains waiting to be dragged into sex parties.

Presumably, after being hosed down - most drains are dank, stinking cesspits.

Doesn't it make perfect sense that a manufacturer makes a bunch of unsellable men's clothes and out of greed, sells them to women?

Unisex my fucking arse.

If it was *real* unisex gear, we'd *all* be wearing bloody caf-tans.

Or boiler suits, bib n brace overalls, or "siren suits," as the fashion was known during the Second World War.

"It's a beautiful place you have here," she said.

"Yes, it is. Thank you."

Though it did feel a bit fraudulent to take the credit for Granny's garden.

She took another sip of her coffee and then abruptly set it down.

"As I said, my daughter's gone missing."

I opened my daybook to the second page, picked up my pen, and not interrupting, prepared to take notes.

"I tried calling the Police, but they said she was an adult and could come and go as she saw fit."

"While it's true she's an adult with free will, if you're concerned about her, you should go into a Police station to report her missing, in person, as soon as possible."

She pulled a crumpled tissue from the sleeve of her jacket and dabbed her glistening eyes, "I ordered our usual dinner from Golden Shell Chinese - satay chicken skewers, mandarin pork, black pepper steak, garlic prawns, and large fried rice. She went to pick it up and didn't come back."

Strangely specific about the order.

I compared her to Mother.

We didn't usually see eye to eye about anything.

Agreeing to sit down to eat would be difficult enough, let alone agreeing on what kind of food, which restaurant and the actual dishes.

In fact, Mother'd more or less blackmailed me into attending twenty-six functions over the year. Once a fortnight, I get dressed up and follow her to Gallery openings, gala dinners and balls.

Who'd've guessed we'd never bloody run out of events?

Things I do for a quiet life.

I couldn't imagine anyone willingly spending time with their female parental unit.

"We're very close you see," she said, as if sensing my doubt. "She's always dropping by, or we're chatting on the phone. Some contact every day."

I suppressed another shudder as I thought about her spider-like walk again.

Did you know that most spiders are generally *very* protective of their babies, known as spiderlings, until they're old enough to leave home?

They lay their eggs in a sack and carry it close.

Wolf spiders, for example, are wanderers who carry their egg sacks with them. When the eggs hatch, they carry their spiderlings on their backs until they're ready to parachute away to the ground.

Orb spiders, on the other hand, abandon their egg sacks in trees, leaving the spiderlings to fend for themselves.

Mind you, Orb mummies eat their babies' daddies too.

And their webs are strong enough to capture small humans.

Mother is most definitely Orb-like.

The Wolf-woman sniffed, then blew her nose, "the Police asked if I gave her any money, as if that was the only time I ever saw her."

"And did you?"

"Not really."

I took a sip of coffee, almost poking my eye out with the pen.

"Just fifty bucks to go pick up the takeout we ordered."

I nodded and made a note.

Fifty bucks was cheap for that amount of food - I'd be expecting something closer to seventy-five or eighty.

"That was three days ago. I tried calling her, but the phone went to voice mail. I went to her flat, and the mail's still in the box."

"And her car?"

"She took it to go get the takeout."

I made another note, "what did the restaurant say?"

"She didn't get there."

"Is it far away?"

"Just a couple of minutes by car."

I scratched my head with the pen as I thought, "have you walked the route she would've taken?"

"I thought the Police would've done that, but I guess they haven't."

"Do you have a Police report number?"

She shook her head, frowning. "I can't believe I'm so stupid. They're not going to do anything are they?"

"Did you go into a station to formally report her missing? They can't investigate if you don't."

She dabbed her eyes again, "I'm not sure they even believed she's my actual daughter."

It didn't sound like she was even listening to me.

Nonetheless, I could sort it out. At least, I was pretty sure I could.

"So, I charge fifty dollars an hour, plus any expenses. And I'm also going to need a five-hundred-dollar deposit."

I felt grimy talking about money in the face of her grief, but after my office got blown up...

Then again, I haven't fully developed my psycho/time-waster exclusion process, but the "extortionate" deposit's working well so far.

She pulled out her phone, "your transfer identification?"

And two minutes later, a ping announced another payment.

Yay!

But...

Wasn't she being a bit hasty? The Police find missing persons for free.

Well, that is eventually they find missing persons, so I suppose payment me is a few steps faster.

She took a long shaky sigh. "I don't care how much it costs; I just need to find her. It doesn't matter whether she comes back or not, I just need to know she's okay."

Yeah, like whatever.

Perhaps better to give the money to me than some "Nigerian Prince" who'd just waste it on drugs and loose women.

Then again, in a recent documentary, I discovered for most scammers, it's just a day job, working minimum wage, nine to five in an office for "the man."

"The man" being the gutless, self-serving, unappreciative boss/supervisor who sets unrealistic targets in a bit to rake in shit loads of stolen cash for a criminal kingpin.

Mainly because they get a cut of the action.

Which is also why they pay minimum wage.

Or worse, the scammers could be slaves, trafficked from the other side of the planet. Their lives depending on meeting their targets.

But, back to the case at hand, why was she avoiding going to a Police station?

As well as her contact information, I took the details the Police would ask for.

What did her daughter look like, were there any distinguishing features?

What was her health like and was she taking any medications?

Her home address, and place of work.

The make, model and registration of her car.

The clothes she was wearing the last time she was seen.

The restaurant she was supposed to be collecting the food from.

The names and addresses of her friends, and the names of any new people in her life.

A picture of a laughing, red-headed young woman.

Clearly the mother's daughter.

And finally, the spare key to her apartment.

"I really do think it's important you go back to your local Police station to lodge a missing person's report."

She grimaced.

It wasn't like I could make her.

Still mystified by why she'd pay me to investigate when the Police would do it for free?

She looked like she could barely afford the deposit.

I stood up, "well, I think that's enough for me to get started with."

"Thank you. When do you think you'll have something for me?"

I glanced at my watch out of habit, not because I was expecting a speedy resolution, "I'll be back in touch as soon as I have anything, and if I don't have anything, I'll be back in touch when the retainer runs out."

"Thank you," she said again, standing, walking around the table, reaching out to shake my hand, "you come highly recommended and I can't tell you how relieved I am that you're on the case."

Recommended by whom? Though I didn't care enough to ask.

I smiled slightly, and gestured to the door leading to the stairs and elevator.

She took the hint and left.

4

After the morning's crime-busting exercise, I couldn't be bothered going out, or talking to more people, again so soon.

So, I cleared the dishes away and settled on the couch with my laptop.

Turned the TV onto some reality show or other for a bit of noise.

And stretched, luxuriating, for a just moment, in the pleasure of having brand new furniture and appliances, in a nice, new and most delightful of all, clean apartment, in a new building.

Possibly made of second-hand materials.

Then got back to business.

Opened a new file and labelled it Wolf and Orb.

Sent Wolf my conditions of engagement along with a receipt.

Then cruised through Orb's social media accounts.

She hadn't posted anything for three days.

Which lent some credence to Wolf's story.

Because you have to assume your client's story is on the more true than less side of the equation.

Looked further back.

Orb was a frequent poster, often several times a day.

Look at me being pretty in the park in my new top/jeans/shoes!

Look at me having a delicious lunch at the latest restaurant/café/snack bar!

Look at me and my besties at some hotel/bar/club!

Someone with that level of engagement rarely has the strength to quit cold turkey.

I wondered if she was a sponsored influencer, and if so, by whom.

Where she was tagged, I slipped across to look at her friends' feeds.

Orb had a fairly long presence on their feeds, with no sign of concern about her whereabouts. Though of course, they could all be influencers who met regularly just to take the pictures.

I cross-checked Orbs friends against Wolf's list, and there were a few she hadn't mentioned.

Couldn't at this stage say whether Wolf knew about them, or just didn't approve of them.

Debated with myself about contacting those of Orb's friends her mother had known about, just to suss them out.

It would be quicker and easier to direct message them, what with not having to get off the couch, but you get a lot more information when you see them in person.

Plus, you get to see their reactions as you question them.

Went back through Orbs accounts and isolated the three most common taggers to follow up with first.

When I went out to interview them, I'd ask them to contact her to see what happened. Would they have more or less success than Wolf or me?

Maybe they could post missing notices on their feeds as well.

I tried Orb's phone and as Wolf said, it went to voice mail.

I left a message, because you never know.

"Hi! My name is Georgia Garside. I'm the private investigator your mother hired to find you. She's worried about you and wants to make sure you're okay. If you don't want to talk to her, please call me and I'll let her know."

And then for good luck, I texted an abbreviated version as well.

Plugged the number into a phone tracker, which told me she was in Canberra.

Not necessarily significant, her phone company was possibly based in Canberra, using that location as an anti-stalker mechanism.

Then again. Canberra is about a day's drive from Melbourne, and it was possible she'd driven there voluntarily, but you had to ask why?

Sure, it's Australia's capital, and the national universities, museums and galleries are there, but it's mainly the place where public servants live, and not much more.

In the usual scheme of things, the only reasons I'd go there was if I was on a case, I'd followed my one true love (snort), or been kidnapped.

Though I once visited an excellent Italian restaurant while I was in the region.

So, not beyond the realms of possibility, but unlikely she'd driven there voluntarily.

Unless she'd been car-jacked.

Also not beyond the realms of possibility.

And assuming she or her phone was actually in Canberra.

Checked the Missing Person's Database to find she wasn't in it.

While it's coordinated by the Australian Federal Police, the only way to get in it, is to go to your local Police Station to file a missing person's report.

Theoretically, anyone who has concerns for someone's welfare or safety can file a missing person's report.

But as I'd just been engaged, I wasn't that concerned about her yet.

There were still a lot of other avenues to investigate before I'd be concerned enough to report her missing.

And, at least according to her mother, she was in perfect health with no medical conditions or medications to be worried about.

Though I did call the major Melbourne hospitals, asking whether Orb (in particular) had been admitted.

And when the answer came back no, whether any unidentified women had been admitted.

Also no.

That, at least, was good news!

5

The next morning, after I'd crowbarred Binky off me, I decided to visit Orb's apartment.

Dressed in nice practical black jeans, a long-sleeved black t-shirt, and my red sneakers.

I want to point out, that they were not the same black jeans, t-shirt or sneakers I was wearing the day before. Like most Melbournites, I have many pairs of black jeans and t-shirts.

Though I only have two pairs of the exact same red sneakers, so I can let them air out for a day between wears.

I'm sure I don't need to tell you why.

Added a black lightweight backpack and got on a tram.

Not entirely sure whether Wolf had entered the apartment, but given there was still mail in the box in the foyer, perhaps not.

First, check the security office to find out when Orb was last there.

Except, the office was closed, with no indication that it was actually staffed. Fair enough, this wasn't the kind of high-end building you'd expect to find a concierge service.

Picked up the mail, took the elevator to the fifth floor, and entered the tiny apartment.

As I opened the door, the air was cold and a little damp, smelling stale and musty. As though no one had visited for several days.

Something else to add in favour of Wolf's time line.

To my right was a large open room with a tiny galley kitchen at the inside edge, the rest nominally split into dining and lounge by a round, flat pack four-seater table and couch. Though a large sliding door at the other end, I could see a balcony.

And a bucket of cigarette butts.

To my left, a tiny, enclosed bathroom, with a small drying rack of female undies pegged out inside the shower enclosure. No lingering smell of shampoo or detergents.

By deduction, the pocket door on the left at the far end of the living room led to the bedroom.

All nicely decorated with the rental standard colours of beige, mushroom and sandy off—white.

Pulled out my phone and took a few snaps as a memory refresher.

It wasn't display home clean and clutter-free, but neither was it the kind of messy you expect a home that's been turned over by thieves to be.

At the first glance, just kind of lived in.

A knife and teaspoon, plain white bread plate and mug in the sink.

Crumpled burger takeout bag on the floor by the bin.

Though no aromas of toast or burger lingered in the air.

A pile of odd bits and pieces on the table as though someone had emptied their handbag onto it.

Robe thrown across the foot of the bed.

But at the same time, it wasn't particularly homely. No pictures on the wall, no photos on the chest of drawers

In fact, I'd have laid money that it was transitory accommodation. The kind of place you take by the day.

Which would make it more along the lines of a cut-price hotel or badly maintained home stay than a residential apartment.

I shuffled through the mail, sorting the junk mail to the back of the pile, leaving six envelopes addressed to six different names.

None of which belonged to Orb.

Shoved the mail in my bag while I checked the wardrobe to find no clothes in it.

No clothes in the drawers either.

Or anything else for that matter.

Went back to the beginning and checked the kitchen cupboards - just generic white crockery, some with the Made in China stickers still attached.

Generic pots and fry pans, but no baking dishes or casseroles.

Mostly empty container of cheap dish washing liquid and a worn sponge with the scourer mostly torn off.

Nothing in the bin.

The tablet of soap in the bathroom was dry and cracking.

A single sheet of toilet paper left on the roll, no spares tucked into the bathroom cupboard.

This place was clearly not Orb's home.

Was Wolf aware her daughter slept at a different address?

Was Wolf Orb's mother?

On a whim, I caught the elevator down to the basement car park and strolled through three levels of sparsely filled car park.

Just when I was starting to think my imagination was running overtime, I found the car.

Gun metal grey, plain standard wheel rims, no stickers or other distinguishing features.

Neatly parked as if nothing untoward was going on.

No tickets under the windshield wipers.

It didn't appear to have been involved in any kind of incident; just the usual kind of scrapes and scratches you'd expect of a modest ten-year-old sedan.

The keys were in the ignition, hanging on a tag advertising hire cars.

I pressed my lips together as the hairs on the back of my neck lifted.

This was starting to feel a little familiar.

Nonetheless, I stuffed my hands in the pockets of my jeans as I leaned towards the car, squinting as I tried to look through my reflection to the interior.

Which was just the same kind of lived in as the apartment.

A half empty soft drink bottle in the passenger footwell.

A nondescript dark blue denim jacket thrown across the back seat. Impossible to tell whether it belonged to a man or a woman.

I walked away.

Too late to take any defensive action.

I hadn't looked for security cameras, but'd most likely been caught on them taking the mail from the communal box, and then approaching the apartment.

Most likely been captured on video leaving the apartment, then looking at the car.

Most assuredly had left the mail with my finger prints on it inside the apartment.

And if anything came of my little visit to the apartment, at least I had detailed notes of Wolf's visit and financial records to prove I was on a legitimate investigation.

6

I stopped at a café in a building diagonally across from the apartment. Ordered a large latte and a vanilla slice. Sat in the window to watch what happened over the road.

Had no idea what I was looking for, but I was pretty sure I'd know if I saw it.

Took out my daybook and started writing.

The main question on my mind was whether Orb was missing or not.

Supplementarily, was she the person whom I'd been ostensibly hired to find, or was Orb a *nom de guerre*, hiding her true identity.

Perhaps an undercover police officer or journalist, or maybe a stripper or some kind of sex worker.

Further, was Wolf the mother she'd claimed to be, someone unrelated who *was* concerned, or someone else who'd unlawfully detained Orb.

Like a brothel keeper.

And if Orb was missing, had she escaped from Wolf to freedom, or been trafficked somewhere worse.

It seemed sensible to assume Wolf had known I would visit the apartment, and if it turned out she was a criminal

37

mastermind, I could expect to see the trap closing around me.

Which by that point is what I was expecting to see as I watched the apartment building across the road.

Several hours later, after ordering an additional coffee, and a little later a small pizza, I decided I was safe for the moment.

Not that the Police (etc.) couldn't have just as easily come and gone though the goods and services entrance and escaped my attention, but that I hadn't seen the kind of activity that would suggest site visits of any kind of investigation.

What I had seen, was a lot of coming and going of international students.

It occurred to me, that depending on class schedules and work shifts, it would be possible for several students to share a one-bedroom apartment.

Or prostitutes.

Though I'd've thought an active brothel would've smelled more like soap, and had a bin full of condoms.

While Orb's apartment hadn't smelled as though anyone had visited it recently, it was entirely possible it was only used as a place to "safely" have sex.

I was starting to wish I'd opened the letters.

I started packing up my things, and rediscovered them in my bag.

In Australia, it is an offence to open mail that's not addressed to you.

We all tend to assume everything in our mail boxes is for us.

So, people open mail that's not addressed to them all the time.

Like when it's sent to your address in error, delivered to your place by accident, or doesn't have a name on the envelope.

As long as you send it back or redeliver to the proper address; you're fine.

But.

Stealing mail and intentionally opening it is an offence, punishable by up to five years imprisonment.

It'd be foolish, as well as six offences, to open six envelopes addressed to six different people I'd taken from a mailbox that wasn't mine...

Especially given the potential of video footage of me taking it...

And the potential of being caught up in an elaborate sting...

Not to mention having my private investigations license cancelled followed by five years exclusion after being released from prison.

And lord knows I didn't want the Australian Federal Police looking into me if I was going to end up reporting Orb missing.

I looked through the envelopes to see what I could make out through them.

Which wasn't much given the address details were well spaced and enclosed in patterned security print.

Got out my phone, did a quick internet search on the GPO Box return address to discover it was the Department of Immigration and Citizenship.

Tapped my phone against my lip.

Very interesting.

Wrote the addressee names in my daybook.

Did a quick title search on the apartment, paid the fee, refreshed my email until the results came in.

Lightning Unit Trust.

So. The apartment was owned by a kind of joint venture where each unit holder was entitled to a specific amount of the capital and income invested in the trust.

Was it a coincidence Orb worked for a company called Lightning Advisory Services?

But was the apartment the only asset the trust had invested in, or was it also, for the sake of argument, six people with letters from the Immigration Department.

And was it a legitimate enterprise, or was it the kind where you took a job, the company applied for a visa for you, and you ended up somewhere else entirely as a drug addicted sex slave whose passport had been confiscated by the brothel keeper.

I considered my options.

I had been engaged to find the woman who allegedly lived at the address.

A woman whose name was not represented in the envelopes.

Could I lawfully return the envelopes to the Department on the assumption the apartment was rented by Orb?

It seemed as though the right thing to do by all those people, assuming they existed, was to return them.

With a cover letter, or loose?

Perhaps the proper thing to do was to send a cover letter, but I didn't really want to get involved in an immigration enquiry.

Scrawled Return to Sender Not at This Address on the envelopes, took a photo of them.

Finished packing, started walking down Elizabeth Street and dropped the envelopes in the first box I came across.

Took a photo to remind me which one it was, should the matter come up for hypothetical future discussions with assorted police departments.

Kept walking down Elizabeth Street at a fair clip, towards the Collins Street address Wolf had given me for Orb's work address.

I didn't hold out much hope.

7

There didn't seem much point in trying to conceal my movements, but I paused here and there, looking in the glass windows to see if anyone was following me.

Nothing obvious.

The building Lightning Advisory Services, and Orb, supposedly worked in was a thirteen-story, mostly glass clad office building at the eastern so-called "Paris end" of Melbourne near the Victorian Parliament.

Known as the Paris end due to its heritage buildings, street trees, and street cafés.

Not to mention all the high-end Paris brands with stores at that end.

In terms of offices, it was a good central location with train, trams and buses close by. Not to mention loads of Government Departments.

Though not (currently) Immigration and Citizenship, which was located closer to the apartment.

I took the elevator up to the fifth floor.

It was a clear, light filled office with new grey carpet tiles, laid in a chequerboard pattern, still fragrant with carpet adhesive.

Patterned glass divided the floor into meeting rooms and offices, some painted white, and with attractive wood effect floorboard panels fixed to the walls.

Even better, the floor had windows that actually opened *as well* as centralised air conditioning.

But it was completely empty - no desks, no filing cabinets, and most tellingly no people.

I went back downstairs and located the security office.

A passably attractive, largish and seemingly well muscled, black haired, black suited man was sitting behind a reception counter, talking on the phone.

The opaque wall behind him contained a beige door and a whiteboard with names, little red magnets marking them in or out.

The room smelled of testosterone.

Not that I know what testosterone smells like, except perhaps football locker rooms, or any other rooms where predominantly men work.

He dropped the phone in its cradle and frowned up at me.

"I'm looking for Lightning Advisory Services? Supposed to be on level five?"

"Lightning Advisory Services? Not sure we have one of those. Let me check."

He typed impressively fast into a concealed computer, "ahh. Nope, never had a company by that name here."

I gave him Orb's name.

He typed again, "we haven't issued a security card by that name."

It was a long shot, but I showed him the picture Wolf had given me.

"She looks familiar... May I?"

I wasn't happy about it, but I handed over my phone.

Fortunately, he set it up on the desk, where we could both see it, and typed a bit on his computer.

Muttering to himself as he searched.

"Not exactly the same," he said, "but very close."

He beckoned me around the side of the counter to look at the computer, "here, look at this."

I was pretty sure it was the same young woman, though this time with mousy brown hair. Perhaps a little older, or a little more worn down with life.

"Dianne Smith," he clicked on her image, "she's a cleaner, subcontracted by..." his finger traced over the screen. "FireBolt Resourcing. Last date she was here..." more finger tracing, "three days ago."

That at least was consistent with the story.

It didn't escape my attention that FireBolt might be related to Lightning.

Because even though the words were different, they more or less meant the same thing.

Not exactly damning, but it did make the hair on the back of my neck stand up.

Again.

"Could I get a copy of the photo?"

"Sure," he printed it out, handing it over with my phone, "hope you find her."

Odd thing to say.

"Thanks," I said, and left.

Pausing to wait for a traffic light to change, I compared Dianne Smith's photo with Orb's again.

They were very similar...

A few blocks further down Collins Street, I stopped to look at my phone.

It *looked* fine.

But.

I'd been watching a lot of foreign TV recently including a French crime drama in which a criminal kingpin named Didier has corrupt people planted everywhere.

Okay, not all corrupt, more like people who are in desperate circumstances looking for an "angel" to pay off all their debts, get their kids into good schools, or sick parents/wives/husbands into good hospitals.

He "invested" in you, and then a bit later, he'd ask you for a favour. The kind of favour that seemed like a faceless, victimless crime.

They were all the kind of people you'd never expect to be caught up in something of dubious lawfulness.

Like passably attractive well muscled, black haired, black suited, men behind security counters.

It had seemed perfectly innocent to put my phone on the reception desk where it could be clearly seen.

But, had there been some kind of device under the desk to clone it, or wipe it, or track its use.

Which led me to the horns of a dilemma.

Since my previous office had been blown up, I'd started backing up my phone and laptop to a secure, encrypted, two-factor authenticated, cloud server every day.

Authorising only the devices I was currently using, plus one other I kept off-site in a secret location.

Along with my weekly hard drive back up.

So, I could easily restore last night's back up...

But I'd lose the day's photos of the apartment, the envelopes and the mailbox.

Not too concerned about my search results as I'd written down all the pertinent details, though if the phone had been cloned, "they'd" be able to view them.

Mind you, I always open a new tab for each search, and close it down when I'm done, which I imagined would remove the records.

And both Bluetooth and WiFi are set by default to off, just relying on my carrier's routing.

I don't carry my life on my phone either, only one page of relevant and useful apps.

No banking or social media. Just the weather and public transport apps. And the load of shit the phone install comes with.

Easy to see the phone didn't have any apps that weren't there before I handed it over.

It was possible I was being paranoid.

But, as Heller wrote in *Catch 22*, "Just because you're paranoid doesn't mean they aren't after you."

Backtracked to a camera store, queued timestamped print versions of the day's photos.

Reset the phone to factory settings, planning to restore the back up when I got home.

Popped open the SIM card tray with a safety pin.

Went outside to drop the phone, SIM card and tray on the pavement.

Ground the SIM card and tray under my foot.

Picked up the phone, SIM pieces, and photos.

Trotted a couple of blocks to Bourke Street to a phone store for my carrier.

Got a new SIM and bought a replacement tray.

The reset, new SIM and restoring last night's back up ought to take care of any tracking or cloning issues.

Fingers crossed I wouldn't need to get a new phone as well!

I know, I know.

I was refusing to consider Wolf (or someone) had planted a stooge inside the phone store.

Or successfully predicted what actions I might take after visiting the Lightning Advisory Services office.

But the paranoia had to stop somewhere.

Stopped in at a hotel for a stiff drink to consider the results of my investigation so far:

Orb now had two names and two descriptions.

Didn't live at the address given.

Didn't work at the address given.

Didn't perform the role given.

Chances are a visit to the restaurant would not turn out to be her last recorded movements.

Wolf had said she didn't get to the restaurant, but by this point there was no point taking anything she said as true.

Or even factual.

Assuming my phone was now "safe" I looked up the Golden Shell.

Came up with two responses; one in the "correct" suburb but at a different address, the other with the "correct" address in a different suburb.

Flagged down a cab, and gave the address for the correct suburb.

Asked the cab to wait.

Aware the cab clock was ticking, I asked the harried assistant, "can you tell me if you had a particular order three days ago?"

She looked at me hard, with her inscrutable Asian eyes.

I wondered what she saw in my face.

Eventually, she sighed, "maybe, what was the order?"

I checked my daybook, "satay chicken skewers, mandarin pork, black pepper steak, garlic prawns, and a large fried rice."

"Three days ago? Any idea what time?"

"Dunno. Evening I suppose, given it was for dinner."

"Delivery address?"

"Pick up."

She frowned as she scrolled through whatever the search results were, "nope, nothing. Must be the other one."

Clearly, she was used to mixed up restaurants.

"Okay, thanks," I said, turning to leave.

"Oh. Hang on, wait," I fished my phone out and showed her Orb's photo, "don't suppose you recognise this woman?"

"What are you, a cop?"

"No," I shrugged, "just the private investigator hired to find her."

"Show us your identification then."

I pulled my licence from my wallet and showed her.

"Okay," she beckoned me to show her the phone again, peering over the counter to look closely.

"I don't know, she looks kinda familiar, but I see hundreds of people a day, and she's definitely not a regular."

I nodded, "thanks for your help anyway."

"I hope you find her."

I nodded again, picked up a takeout menu, and left the restaurant.

Back in the cab, I asked to go to the other restaurant.

Giving him the impression I'd got the restaurants mixed up.

He sighed, rolling his eyes, but took me there anyway. When we got there, I let him go.

Went through the same rigmarole.

Got the same answers; to the question of the order, and the photo of Orb.

But this time, I ordered a plate of fried rice with jasmine tea to eat in.

Though I really wanted a couple of beers, but best to wait until I got home.

While I waited, I totted up the cost of Wolf's orders; seventy-five bucks at the first restaurant, and eighty-six at the one I was currently eating in.

So.

I was eating at the wrong restaurant.

Neither of the restaurants had taken the order three days ago.

Neither of them had seen Orb.

The only evidence corroborating Wolf's story was that "Dianne Smith" had purportedly last visited the spurious workplace three days ago.

For what that was worth.

I cocked my head as I stared into space.

Did all private investigators get fake cases, or was it just me?

My shoulders slumped.

Did the blackmailers, fakers and scammers look at my website, decide it was half-arsed enough that I'd be so incompetent they'd never get found out?

Maybe I ought to give up my independence and look for a job working for "the man."

Would I be good enough to get a job at Wilkinson's?

Because as far as I was concerned, the only agency I wanted to work at/with/for was the best, and that was Wilkinson's.

So.

What was my next move?

Paid the bill, got some cat food at a corner store, then got a cab home.

And thought maybe I *should* be working at a corner store...

9

And of course, when I got home, I found someone had trashed my place.

There was a clear and present difference between my own usual messy, just kind of lived in, and cupboards emptied onto the floor, furniture upended, cushions and pillows torn open.

I called the cops.

Acutely aware of the fraudulent investigation I'd been engaged to undertake...

Wondering whether my psycho/time-waster exclusion process needed a bigger deposit.

I needed to work out what had been taken, knowing it wasn't going to be obvious.

If the thieves were unrelated to the case, they'd be looking for cash, cards and small easily flippable appliances.

If it was related, probably computing, case files and my daybooks.

Which case was the pertinent question. It couldn't be the current one, way to soon to be ransacking my place for evidence.

But first, I had to locate Binky.

Last time I'd seen her, she'd been on the roof, examining the wildlife from a sun-filled vegetable bed.

"Biii-nky," I called, tapping a tin of cat food with a fork, assuming it was a sound she knew and understood.

Aside from the noise of traffic, human conversations, and bird calls, the roof was silent.

"Binky?"

I thought I heard a small cat query behind me.

Turned around to see her hiding under some kind of wide-leaved plant.

Really should ask Gran what they are.

I knelt down, "Binky, it's so good to see you."

She crawled out from under the plant, and came to investigate the tin. Undignified, but I emptied it on the ground because I'd forgotten to bring a bowl.

I'd taken all my bank and identification cards with me, but when I got back in the apartment, I found the bowl of loose change empty.

As I went around, straightening up a little, assessing what was missing, I was also looking for items that hadn't been there before.

Like cameras or bugs hidden in the light shades or curtains. Or new thumb drives, pens or books.

Of course these days, spy cameras are almost impossibly hard to detect micro devices.

Amateurs might use wired devices so I was looking for extra cords as well. Professionals use ones that hijack your WiFi.

The new TV was gone, (of course) some home decora-tive items, and worst of all, my booze!

No beer for me without leaving the house to get it.

But I'd more or less just moved in, so there wasn't much to steal. Given the explosion took everything I owned, there were no jewellery, designer bags or clothing.

My business and private papers, along with my laptop were secured in a locked box hidden in a faux fireplace. I didn't open it, but picking up a broken vase, I could see it hadn't been tampered with.

Chances are, one (or more) of those hidden cameras I hadn't found yet were there to record the location and ac-cess code.

The Police came and went, gave me a report number to go to my insurance company with.

I took my backpack to the pub.

Paranoid again.

10

One of the things I love about my job, or I suppose more correctly my business, is you're always meeting new and interesting people.

Constantly building your body of knowledge, at the same time as you're building a network of people with handy skills you can call on when you need them.

Sometimes they're clients, sometimes witnesses or other technical specialists.

Now and again, they're even the bad guys behind the awful things that happen to the people who hire me.

Or me.

But, you never know when something, or someone is going to come in handy.

Like my friend Minnow.

I met him at Uni.

Doing odd, unlicensed investigations, while he was doing odd hacks and writing malicious code.

A technical, ahem, genius... He was picked up by the Australian Signals Directorate.

Obviously.

Not exactly sure how he ended up working for them instead of in prison for a hundred years, but there you have it.

He's the one who advised me to use a Virtual Private Network, recommending the one he considered the best.

Also cleaning out my cookies regularly, using long character strings as passwords, and never, ever using free public WiFi.

So naturally when I thought my new apartment was under covert surveillance, he was the first person I got in touch with.

"Hey babe," he said.

I stood up to greet him *faire la bise*; touching cheeks with an air kiss, left, right, left.

Perhaps a little pretentious, but he was born in France and emigrated to Australia with his parents when he was young.

But I admit it made me feel sophisticated.

He put his beer on the table and sat down.

Sipping, as I listed my concerns.

"Okay, you're probably fine with the steps you've taken to manage the phone. You could get a burner phone, though it wouldn't have the features you rely on. Or a few spare SIMs, though that won't help with the surveillance."

I nodded, and let out the breath I wasn't aware I'd been holding.

It seems, for the most part, I'm all good with the precautions I'm taking.

Just so long as I don't let my phone out of my hand again.

"As for the apartment, let's go look." He downed his beer, and I struggled to catch up.

I think it's because bloke's mouths are bigger they can drink faster.

And eat bigger burgers.

But I was thankful I'd bought a couple of long necks while I waited for him.

"Oh my god that's insane," he said as we approached the building, "does your Gran have access to a time machine? It's, like, the same building!"

I grinned, "I know right?"

We caught the elevator up, "you'll need to check the access cards for the lift, make sure they're all accounted for, and that they're only programmed for the floors they're meant to have access to."

"Okay," I nodded.

"Where does the camera feed go to?"

"Um, not sure," shrugging, "I think there's an external service."

"Then you need to check who has access to the feed and the recordings."

He shot me a significant look, "and why were the Police not informed about the unauthorised access?

"Also, can we take a look at the feed to see what the thieves brought with them and took away again? Check how long were they were in the apartment for. What they look like?

"That kind of thing."

I regretted not thinking of all that myself.

In my defence, someone breaking into your apartment takes some of your confidence and thought capacity away.

And I'd already started doubting myself as I'd thought the implication of someone targeting me.

Like perhaps Brown the knife-wielding maniac bomb maker had told Wolf about me?

And not a satisfied customer.

Once we arrived on the top floor, I pushed open the door to the roof, and started walking across to the apartment door.

"Wait," Minnow demanded. "Are you telling me this door isn't even locked?"

I blushed.

He shook his head, "what is the point of me doing anything if you're not going to lock your bloody door?"

I looked at the ground, poking it with a toe, trying to come up with something to say that didn't sound like an excuse.

He fiddled with the door, snibbing the lock to re-engage automatically, "you should get someone here to change all the locks on your level so they can't get in that easily next time."

I started walking towards the apartment again.

"Wait," he said again, "did you check the garden for surveillance?"

I can't believe I hadn't thought of checking the garden either.

I groaned and shook my head.

It wasn't like I was new out of the packet.

Tutting, he pulled some sunglasses from his backpack and slid them on his face before pulling a device out as well.

"Infrared glasses and a radio frequency detector," he said, and started waving the detector around, "I'll leave them with you when I go."

I dropped my bag on the concrete and started following him.

The detector buzzed.

"Got one, come look."

He took a power torch from his bag, "over there," and pointed it at the wall.

He gave me the glasses and device, and I waved it about to hear the different sounds it made.

"The detector finds radio communication frequencies, and the glasses highlight the heat a device is emitting."

I grunted.

"The torch is used to blind the camera, something *you* don't need to do in your own home."

I handed the gear back to him and went to retrieve whatever it was he was pointing at.

"God that's bright," I said shielding my eyes with one hand as I felt around with the other.

"Found something."

"Does it have a wire?"

"I don't think so."

"See if you can find a battery compartment and take the battery out."

I couldn't see anything after being blinded by the light, but managed to get it off the wall.

Prized open something that felt like a ridge, and heard something like a battery plink to the floor.

"Good. No power, no camera, so that's number one down."

I grabbed an empty plant pot (no idea why it was there), chucked the camera in it, and followed Minnow as he continued through the roof garden.

Picking devices off walls, poles and exercise equipment, sickened by how thorough whoever had put them there had been.

I'm pretty sure if all you ever did was install bugs and security cameras you could get it all done in no time, but surely this would've taken at least a couple of hours.

When the outside was done to his satisfaction, we moved inside.

And sure enough, there were cameras in each room.

Including my bedroom, filthy pervs.

And somewhat more worryingly, my office.

Though I did my best work on the couch.

Up yours nasty spying turds!

Oh yeah, there were cameras over the couch as well.

Doh!

"Now, let's look for listening devices. You need to listen for buzzing or beeping, especially around light and power switches.

"Oh, and look for weird lumps in the floor or taped under tables and chairs."

Found a couple in the apartment, but given it was dark, and noisy outside, didn't detect anything there.

"You'll have to sweep a few more times outside, at different times of the day to be sure you've got them all."

He gave me a crooked smile, "in the meantime, maybe don't hold any meetings out here just in case."

I nodded, half smiling, and dusted off my hands.

We went back inside, and Minnow emptied the cameras and recording devices on the table while I poured a couple of beers.

He sorted them out into different sizes and shapes, muttering as he did. "Are you sure it's only one group surveilling you? There's enough different types to make me think there's more."

I shuddered, "fuck's sake that was quick, I just moved in a few weeks ago.

"Well, you will keep on racking up enemies."

I sighed, "so it seems. Friends are too hard to come by."

"So what's the case."

"The latest one's a woman hired me to find her daughter, yet none of the information she gave me seems to be correct."

He smiled, tapping his fingers on the glass, "you know what they say, follow the money. It's always all about the money."

Certainly true in some of my recent cases.

I couldn't help thinking back to my building exploding behind me as I tried to get away.

So neatly imploding, collapsing down around itself, the surrounding buildings were barely affected.

You can't tell me that's not money in action.

I wondered if it was too late to change my speciality, though I had no idea this case would turn into such a cluster fuck.

Hauled the laptop out of its hiding place, logged into my bank to get the deposit details.

Plugged in my phone and restored the backup while I was at it.

Paid by "Lightwing."

A name that called aeroplanes to mind, with a suspiciously coincidental similarity to "Lightning."

Reference "Finders Fee."

Weird, weirder, weirdest.

Wait!

Did that mean "Lightwing," whoever, or whatever that was, had hired more private investigators?

They must want Orb back bad.

But why?

By this point, the only fact of the matter I was sure was true, was that Orb existed.

Perhaps the friendly, curiously unsuspicious, passably attractive, largish and seeming well muscled, black haired security guy was the only one telling the truth.

Was it worth visiting again to confirm his existence?

"Hello! Helloo-oo."

I jumped.

Going by the tone of voice, and the fact of Minnow waving a hand in front of my face, he'd clearly been trying to get my attention for a while.

"Earth to Gee."

I took a big swallow of beer.

Lifting the glass too high and too fast.

Sloshing a good deal of it over my face and down my t-shirt.

Jumped up to grab a tea towel to wipe myself down.

Minnow turned to watch, "so... The money?"

"Lightwing."

"Lightwing?"

"The payment's labelled as a finder's fee from Lightwing."

"That's odd... Let me think a minute."

He was the spy, so it seemed wise to see what he came up with.

...

...

...

"Nah, sorry love," he finished the last of his beer and stood up, "too much brain power expended today, but if I come up with anything, I'll let you know."

I walked him out to the lift foyer, and we did the French kiss thing again.

"Get the locks changed," he said, pointing at the door, "and follow up with the elevator company."

I nodded, smiling as he tested the door to make sure it was locked.

Waited until the elevator arrived, and waved as the doors closed with him in it.

Smiling a little as I considered how he'd grown.

Married with two kids, working in an office, mortgage, local cricket and footy clubs on the weekends.

And I was single, living in a building owned by my grandmother (though I did pay a token rent), not a joiner.

Fairly sure neither of us could have predicted the lives we'd grown into.

11

Back inside, on my own, too wired to sleep, I paced the length of my apartment.

From kitchen to lounge and back again.

Thinking.

About Dianne Smith.

I grabbed the laptop and looked her up.

Found an artist, business lecturer, Associate Professor of Environmental Studies, Chief Executive, Executive Director, Actress, Company Secretary, and Chief Financial Officer, just in the first ten of about twelve and half million results of my search.

No cleaners.

And not counting Di Smith, Diane Smith, Dianna Smith, Diana Smith or other variants thereof.

Nor checking any of the main social media platforms.

It seemed Dianne Smith was a nicely anonymous name.

Too time consuming to properly investigate each one.

Though cleaners aren't generally the kind of people who're well represented on social or any other kind of media.

Middle aged women just getting by the best they can is not glamorous enough for any kind of media coverage.

Then wondered whether she might have some kind of connection with the Lightning Unit Trust. Did FireBolt supply their cleaners?

Most people create names with some sort of significance.

Using family names, as in the Garside Family Trust.

Or names describing the business, like Georgia Garside Investigations.

Others choose something symbolic, like Brainwave Tutoring.

So, why Lightning Unit Trust?

Which called to mind a Norwegian show I'd recently watched, featuring Thor, God of thunder.

Also victory, protection and fair weather for good crops.

Likewise, the Greek god Zeus and Roman Jupiter.

Jupiter was also the god of the Roman army who ruthlessly conquered half the planet.

Back at the laptop I looked up gods of lightning, and found more or less all of them were existential life and death gods.

If they liked you, they protected you, if they didn't, they persecuted you.

Though I suppose most gods did that one way or another.

Or were erratically capricious about it.

If my "lightning bolt" understanding of Orb's apartment as a potential way station for human trafficking was correct...

I shuddered again.

Up until the explosion, I'd considered myself the Robin Hood of private investigation.

Ethical, caring, working for the poor.

And to an extent, I now understood I'd been trying (unsuccessfully), to redefine myself in a way that wouldn't put me in danger.

But Robin Hoods, whatever their names or occupations whether they were police detective John McClane, forensic pathologist Raphaël Balthazar, or Prosecutor Kim Hui Yu, were all ordinary people doing extraordinary things.

Driven to fight injustice.

They didn't let bombs and other threats to their lives stop them from saving the day.

If I did nothing, I was as bad as whoever Wolf was.

Probably the Secretary of the company that owned the Lightning Unit Trust.

Which led me to another set of dilemma horns.

As their hired investigator, I could only collect information relating to Orb's disappearance.

But, as a Licensed Private Investigator, it is an offence to participate in certain kinds of acts.

For example, terrorism, drug trafficking, robbery, or use of controlled weapons.

And by deduction, human trafficking which is bound to be tied up with all that other shit.

I believed Orb existed.

And I believe someone(s) were looking for her.

Orb was someone's daughter, most likely not Wolf. She was entitled to the life of her choosing, no matter how she'd come to the attention of Wolf.

Was looking for the details behind the Trust pertinent to Orb's recovery?

Perhaps tangentially.

I thought about the names on the envelopes; at first glance, not relevant.

But tangentially...

I did not believe Wolf was the mother.

Nor did I believe Wolf had a right to know Orb's whereabouts, aside from the fee given to me.

In terms of lawfully finding Orb, the only leads remaining to me, were contacting her friends, ideally in person.

Trying to find out more about her back story.

But, something about the Lightning Unit Trust was bugging me.

Back to the laptop to see what I could find out.

The unit trust was once owned by a different company, Zhengyi Pty Ltd.

Checked a couple of random translations to find the English equivalent of "justice" and searched for gods of justice, which led me back to Zeus and Jupiter, the pantheon kings of Greece and Rome.

Wasn't that an interesting coincidence?

I didn't think I could ethically charge Wolf the twenty buck fee to search the Australian Securities & Investments

Commission database for details of the current and historical company information of the Lightning Unit Trust.

And the retainer was more or less up anyway.

So I paid for it myself.

Refreshed my email until the link came back.

Followed the link and found the Trust was owned by another company; Inspirit Industries.

Looked up the one listed director, Edward Wenham, and found him employed at a company selling shelf companies.

When shelf companies are sold, they're supposed to be transferred to the new owners, which suggested that this guy was actually running the shelf company, and was therefore the trustee of the Unit Trust.

Or working on behalf of someone(s) who wanted to remain anonymous.

Like human traffickers.

Which reminded me of FireBolt Resourcing, because Dianne Smith was contracted through them.

And I'd already noted the similarity of fire bolts and lightning.

And because it also sounded like a good name for people smugglers.

So I did a quick web search, and discovered it was labour hire for unskilled labourers, including general, construction and demolition labourers, warehouse, factory and gardening labourers, as well as cleaners.

All unskilled work that trafficked people might find themselves indentured to.

And guess who owned it - Inspirit Industries.

So I looked up the ownership of Orb's work address, paying the required fee.

Refreshed my email until I could get at the title deeds.

I'm sure you won't be surprised to learn it was the Lightning Unit Trust.

A definite link between the owner of Orb's apartment and her employers.

I wanted to know more, but didn't know how to go about it.

But, if you want to find out about a corrupt business, isn't the best person to go to, someone who owns a business that skates the fine line between lawful and not?

I sighed, rubbing an eyebrow.

Taipan had technically paid his invoice. And paid for my medical care plus given me a nice settlement as compensation.

I'd fervently hoped never to see him again, aside from Mother's gala dinners etc.

But he was the only one I could ask for help on this.

The Sheriff of Nottingham to my Robin Hood.

I was about ready to call him when I realised it was the middle of the night.

I sighed again, suddenly exhausted, and went to bed.

12

The next morning, I called Taipan's office to make an appointment, and his assistant told me to come by now.

By which I supposed he'd put me on his list of priority contacts, people he'd see when they called.

Without appointments.

Leaving his poor assistant to try and reschedule the rest of his day.

Not that I minded for my sake - the sooner I was out his office the better.

But really, couldn't he at least try to be more considerate of the people he employed.

Then again, I suppose he has a person whose job is exclusively to schedule and reschedule his days.

Poor thing.

I turned up (in black jeans again, because black jeans and t-shirts are about all I own now) and barely had to wait before being called into his office.

He smiled broadly, leaping out of his chair, walking around his desk to shake the hand I reluctantly extended.

"So, have you changed your mind and come to ask for a job?"

Not bloody likely - I'd take a job at the local supermarket before I worked for him.

"Ah, no thanks. I'd like to pick your brain for a moment."

He smiled broadly and popped his head out the door to his assistant, "Hold my calls Judy, and a pot of coffee when you can if you could?"

Which of course meant coffee now and stack of call sheets for later.

"There's no need."

"Nonsense," he said, "Judy makes excellent coffee and I'll need another if I'm going to give you my best advice."

Bloody, bloody, bloody... Fucker.

He strolled across to the conversation setting in front of his desk and sat at its head.

"Any chance I could get an invoice?"

He laughed, gesturing at a chair beside him, "none what so ever, but I'm happy to do you a solid."

Loosely translated as I'll do this for you, and you can pay me back later.

Which is how favours, and criminal kingpins, usually work, but I really didn't want to owe him anything.

Now or later.

Chances are it would escalate.

"So what can I do for you hon?"

Plunking myself into the chair next to the one he'd indicated.

As far away from him as I could get without standing by the door. Ignoring his term of endearment.

I got straight to business.

"Imagine for a moment, you have a drugs business, how would you conceal the fact you owned the business?"

"Ooh, sneaky question. Are you investigating a drugs gang? Isn't that a job for the Police?"

I rolled my eyes, "you know I won't tell you what I'm working on."

"Well, if it involves drugs of any kind, I can tell you, you're in over your head. You should hand your files over to the Police and leave it alone."

"Thanks Dad, just answer the question."

"I—"

Judy picked that moment to wheel in a tray of coffee. With a plate of biscuits. Putting the tray on the conversational setting table.

And leaving.

Perhaps not all that bad a boss if he got biscuits.

And not the cheap shit biscuits I get, but the fancy ones executives get in boardrooms. I couldn't help eyeing off a chocolate coated one.

Dammit.

I waited while he poured the coffee, as he knew I preferred it.

I gritted my teeth.

He suppressed a smile as he slid the cup across to me, then stood and offered me a biscuit.

I closed my eyes and shook my head, but he just waited until I opened them and shook the plate a couple of times in front of me.

Then, when I didn't take one, shook the plate again.

So fucking annoying.

I sighed as I briefly clenched my fists, then fake smiled and took the chocolate coated biscuit I'd had my eye on.

He lifted his cup and took a sip of coffee. "Now then, where were we," he said, tapping his mouth with his index finger.

"That's right, setting up a bunch of fake companies.

"So. Most important thing, open a holding account in a tax haven country that doesn't have any agreements with the Tax Office. Or any other government departments or investigative services."

"But why?"

He laughed, "For starters, you want your money somewhere safe. And you want to make it as complicated to find you as possible. When you go offshore, the Australian jurisdiction ends and it starts getting not only difficult but expensive, because you'd need to hire local investigators to get at the detail."

Difficult and expensive?

Like looking for the right Dianne Smith?

"I see." I said, "and how— "

"You'd need a lawyer or accountant of dubious character for the paperwork, a lot of money, or a patsy to open the account."

"Right, so that's fine, I guess, what's next?"

"Start working back, and confusing the issue in Australia. "These days you need at least one director for a company, and the director must be registered and identified by ASIC."

"Wouldn't that make it difficult?"

"Not if you have money. The easiest way is to buy an existing company and dodge the transfer paperwork."

"But— "

"I think they're cracking down on that, but you could get another patsy here to buy and register the company, while you remain as a "shadow director," controlling the business from the side."

I sipped my coffee, delicious as Taipan had said.

"Plus, ideally, you'd have a tonne of companies owned by other companies, such that it would take you a lot of time and effort to get to the one that's off-shore."

"Isn't that dodgy?"

"Nope, all perfectly legal. Except the bit about the fake directors. All you need to do, is make sure that all your accounts are accurate, fully supported and comply with the relevant legislation. As long as that's all tickety-boo, you're golden."

He took another sip of his coffee, "though if someone gets the accounts mixed up, or you lodge your returns late and someone investigates, then it's likely to come crashing down around you."

Mind you, the owner of any criminal enterprise that doesn't have its own dedicated bookkeeper would have to be nuts. Though how you'd insulate them from the business enough to be sure they didn't have any incriminating evidence was another thing entirely.

But it was enough to be going on with.

I stood up.

He remained seated, but arched an eyebrow, "any company in particular you'd like to investigate?"

Lord knew what that might cost me, but...

There was no way I could get through all that on my own.

Presumably he employed people to research companies full-time.

Not that anyone was going to label their company as "people smuggling," but digging through a succession of interrelated companies was bound to reveal something wasn't it?

I gave in - technically it wasn't case related, "I need to know who's behind the Lighting Unit Trust."

Dumb dumb dummmb.

13

Finally extricating myself from Taipan's clutches, I left him with the promise to return the next day for the search results.

Making an appointment, and hoping his company searcher would not be stuck at work for half the night.

Aimlessly wandered through shops and arcades, trying to get my shit together.

No closer to solving the actual case, I'd been hired to complete.

Unsure whether I should approach Wolf for more money because I had nothing to report.

Not exactly clear about what Taipan could find out about the trust.

Or whether I had anything more than my gut instinct to go on.

But I found myself back at the "Paris-end" of town, looking at the building Dianne Smith (and perhaps Orb) worked in.

I shrugged.

Nothing to lose.

I walked in.

And the passably attractive man was there again.

Which didn't rule out him being beholden to either Wolf, or FireBolt Resourcing.

But did make me feel as through I'd wasted my time and money on the company searches.

"Hello again," he said.

I smiled, "I wondered if I could ask you a few more questions?"

"Shoot."

"Does the building use FireBolt for more than cleaning?"

"Sure, we... They also do the security for the building."

"And have you noticed any... Irregularities in dealings with them?"

"No, but I just work here," he said, pointing at the desk. "If there were any issues, they wouldn't come to me they'd go to head office.

"Anyhow, the cleaners come in as a group with their own supervisors so I would've thought the cleaners could take up any issues they had with them."

Ah bless. The little fucker didn't have any idea how the world really worked.

"Can you tell me how long Dianne Smith has been working here?"

He wheeled himself closer to his computer, and started typing, "Let's see... Her security pass was issued twelve years ago."

Twelve years?

How was that possible?

"With the same pass all that time?"

He laughed, "goodness no - a card wouldn't last that long. They wear out after a couple of years so we take new pictures when the new ones are issued.

Right then, relatively recent picture.

"Is there anyone who checks the people in?"

"Nah, all automatic. They're not suppose to swap their cards with anyone else, so if you have a card, you can get in.

"I suppose we rely on the supervisors to make sure they have the right people with them."

I managed not to roll my eyes, but his lumbering intellect did reduce his attractiveness.

Not to worry, I had enough information for the time being anyway.

"Thanks for your help."

"No worries, anything else feel free to come back."

I suppose that partially explained why he hadn't asked why I was asking these questions, and under what authority was I asking them.

Fairly glad he wasn't the concierge of my building.

Not that there is one.

Though I suppose, technically, it's me.

With nothing more to do just then on the case, I went shopping.

I needed a new TV.

And a toothbrush.

Just in case...

14

The next morning, I was back in Taipan's building. Catching the lift up to the top floor executive suite.

I think it's hubris that the Chair and Chief Executive are literally located on the top floor of buildings, *because* they're at the top of the hierarchy.

When you get down to it, they're the *foundation* of a company, and should be in the basement. If they're honest and ethical, the company is too.

But if they're not... Well, neither is the business.

I think Taipan is dishonest.

He works within the letter of the law, but not always the spirit of it. His intentions, decisions and consequent actions are not always moral.

Though I suppose he works according to some kind of strange moral code that ordinary mortals do not.

Perhaps that's what makes him such a successful businessman - ultimately, he decides what he wants and then acts accordingly.

Perhaps he hires with that in mind, and only hires people as driven as he is.

Which is why I will probably never be rich.

Though really, what is the actual point of being rich?

Taipan, as usual, was immaculately dressed in a bespoke suit.

I suppose that's one reason to be rich.

And as the equally immaculate Judy arrived with a trolley of coffee and biscuits shortly after me, perhaps proof of his hiring criteria.

He came to shake my hand, drenching me in the musky scent of his cologne, "there you are!"

God he was laying it on a bit thick.

The search results must have been good to greet me with that amount of enthusiasm.

I dropped into the chair I'd sat in the day before and helped myself to another chocolate biscuit.

I had the feeling I was going to need it.

He poured me a coffee and handed it over before pouring himself one.

Grinning, he sat next to me, instead of the seat at the head of the small table.

I have him a hard stare, but dammit, my lips twitched. "I take it you have good news?"

"Of course," he took a sip of coffee then put the cup down and handed me a manilla folder stuffed with sheets of paper that had been sitting on the table.

"What's this?"

"The search results."

I flopped the file a couple of times to see the papers fan, glimpsing the dense type.

"Don't just look at it, *read* it!"

Rolling my eyes, I sculled the coffee, burning the back of my throat, and put the cup down.

Opened the folder to see the initial Lightning Unit Trust search I'd done. And the next page was for another company owned by Inspirit.

And another. Another and another.

And then the report for Inspirit.

Owned by another company.

A bunch of companies owned by that company.

Including Lightwing Engineering.

More and more interlinked companies.

That poor company searcher must have been there half the night to come up with such a huge stack of paper.

The interesting thing though, was Edward Wenham, the shelf company reseller kept coming up.

And his name was not the only one.

The other was Dianne Smith.

Which *might* have been a coincidence.

But thinking about the criteria of making the searches time and money consuming.

And thinking about the similarity of Orb and Dianne Smith's photos again.

Was it possible Orb and Wolf were the same person?

The same person as Dianne Smith in fact.

Had Wolf asked me to investigate herself, thinking an investigation might free her from whatever situation she'd got herself into?

I screwed up my face.

No, she wouldn't have.

Would she?

It was possible Orb was about the same age as Dianne Smith, but Orb had been much younger.

"Do you by any chance know Dianne Smith?"

Taipan sputtered, "why would you think that?"

"I don't know how it works; you're a Chief Executive, she's a Company Secretary, maybe you meet at seminars or networking functions or something?"

He thought about it for a moment, "well, I did know a Dianne Smith at University, but she dropped out and we didn't stay in touch. I haven't met a Dianne Smith related to any of these companies."

It was a one in a billion chance, but I took out my phone and showed him the photo of Orb.

"Oh my god, that's her! Where did you get this?"

I shook my head, this was surreal.

I took out the photo of Dianne, "do you think this could be the same person?"

"Mmmm. I'd say so, but life sure hasn't been kind to her."

"This is a photo of Dianne Smith. She's a labour hire cleaner employed by FireBolt Resourcing.

"Ah. The perfect patsy."

Judy knocked on the door and walked in, heading straight to Taipan, whispering in his ear.

He got up and walked to his desk, grabbed a remote and pointed it at his wall of cabinets.

The doors retracted to reveal a TV which turned on at a news channel.

The video footage showed the Police pulling a body from the Yarra, switching to a view of ambulance officers pushing a covered body on a trolley to an ambulance. The body's face was concealed.

I stood horrified as the voice over rolled on, "… in Fairfield, near the Fairfield Park Boathouse. The body has been identified as fifty-two-year-old Company Secretary Dianne Smith. She hadn't married and leaves no dependants…"

The footage reverted to a montage of photos, of the woman at various company publicity events; signing agreements, handing over large novelty cheques, ground breaking ceremonies.

The woman was clearly Dianne Smith the cleaner.

We looked at each other, and Taipan said, "I think we've found your patsy."

I dialled Wolf's number.

It rang and rang and rang before cutting out.

No voice mail.

Odd these days, but not unknown.

The news channel was going on about Dianne's sudden death, replaying the same footage over and over.

"… it's not yet clear whether the death is the result of suicide, murder, or she just fell into the river and drowned.

Dianne Smith is the sixth unexplained death since Tuesday..."

"Do you have your story straight?" Taipan asked.

"Story, what story?"

"Well, clearly she knew something was about to go down and wanted you to investigate her. Which you did, so I'd lay odds the shadow director murdered her."

"But we don't know who the shadow director is!"

"Doesn't matter, we've collected enough information to convict Edward Wenham, assuming he's survived the purge."

"Purge?"

"Oh come on Bubba Gee," he said, referring to my childhood nickname.

I half-heartedly aimed a karate chop at him.

"You're smarter than this. You know that sooner or later you're going to have to give all your work to the Police."

I dialled again, and after a bit, a male voice answered, "Dianne Smith's phone, who's calling?"

I didn't say anything.

The man said, "this is Detective Sergeant Nate Stone, who is this?"

Detective Sergeant Nate Stone, my law-abiding nemesis.

He'd been in charge to the investigation into the explosion of my building, for which I'd been the chief suspect.

When they investigated my stabbing, the case had been rolled into the bomb investigation, and even though I'd been cleared, he was still treating me like a suspect.

As if I'd arranged the stabbing to clear my name!

I sighed.

No escaping it now.

Even if I hung up, they'd trace the call and get back to me.

"This is Private Investigator Georgia Garside. I was investigating a missing person's case for Ms Smith."

Taipan patted my back.

15

I gave the detestable Detective Sergeant Nate Stone my statement.

He spent too much time criticising the quality of my case notes, and not enough time appreciating the amount of time it saved his team.

I suppose that's the typical relationship between Police Officers and Private Investigators.

Though I hope some of them somewhere in the real world are as collegiate in their approaches as some of them are in TV land.

There are some things we can do better than them, given we're never swamped by the press of investigations the way they are.

Or the press for that matter.

And after that, I heard nothing about the investigation.

I suppose that's also the usual way.

With no next of kin, Wolf was cremated and scattered in the crematorium ash pit as soon as the Police finished their investigation.

A fact I discovered by reading the tabloid newspapers as was my custom.

Someone organised a small memorial for her, at Altona Memorial Park's Chapel of Peace (also something I read in the papers), and I went along.

A surprisingly small affair.

Though the scandal had broken by then and people were swearing they'd never met her for more than five minutes.

Even more surprising, Taipan and Minnow took the time to attend as well.

And hey, no one had tried to kill me this time. At least not yet.

Except that half hearted teenage bag snatcher and for these purposes it doesn't count.

Months later, what sounded like a work experience Police Officer called me to let me know the murderer had been caught.

And they'd be retaining my case files for Court.

And a bit later, to ask when I could collect them, (because I am required to retain them for a minimum period of five years).

I don't know how she faked the social media platforms for Orb.

The same way I would I suppose, find a wunderkind to fake it for me.

And as a fake Company Director, I guess she came across a few of them.

I'm not sure why she kept her cleaning pass alive for so long. Perhaps because it was something to fall back on.

Which reminds me.

I need to get the locks changed,
And take another run at my psycho exclusion process.
But that's another story...

95

THE END

As a small token of my thanks for reading...
Please enjoy 10% off everything (excluding shipping)
at alexandriablaelock.com
with the code binky10.
Turn the page for some ideas where to use it...

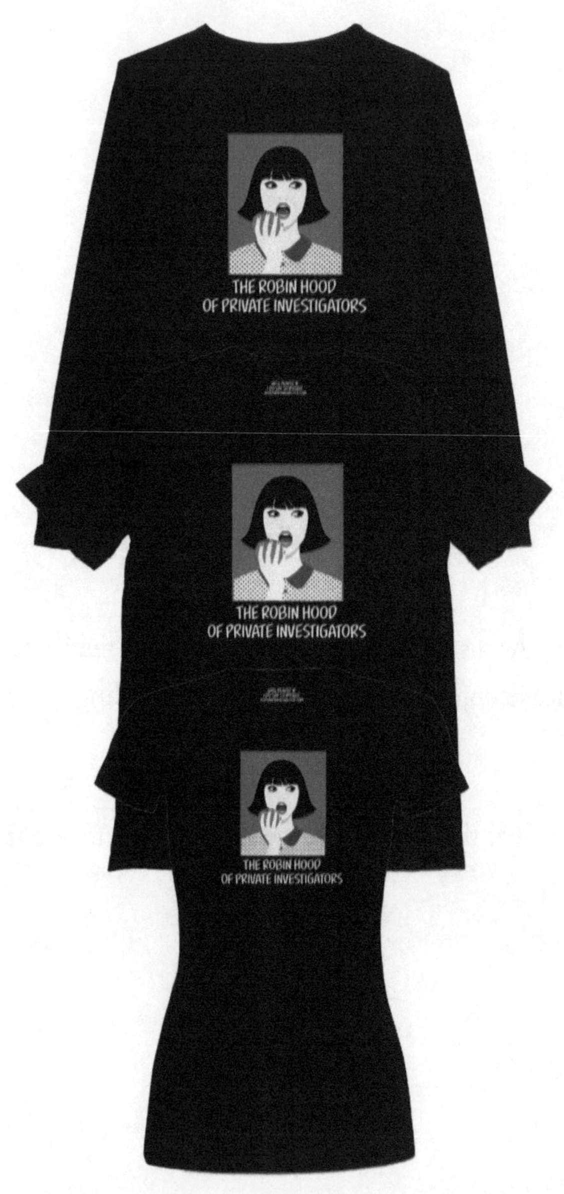
THE ROBIN HOOD
OF PRIVATE INVESTIGATORS

THE ROBIN HOOD
OF PRIVATE INVESTIGATORS

THE ROBIN HOOD
OF PRIVATE INVESTIGATORS

MORE RELATED MERCHADISE

The Robin Hood of Private Investigators.

Georgia Garside. Foul-mouthed Private Investigator.
Ex-contorionist.
Out of her depth. In over her head.
Caught up in the war between a wealthy industrialist
and the ex-sugar babe who can't take a hint.
A laugh-out-loud tripartite battle of wits, winner
takes all.

One good turn deserves another
Ellie Porterfield is not one of THE Porterfields though she works in high-end fashion at their department store.

When a severely beaten man collides with her at a bus stop she calls an ambulance and renders first aid.

Is drawn further into a web of danger and deceipt that could cost her life.

But could it shed light on her troubled past as well?

Welcome to Wilkinson's

I'm afraid Mr Hall's running a little late, can I get you a tea or coffee while you wait?

No?

What if I tell you about some of the recent cases we've been involved in?

Yes?

Then get comfortable and settle in for a wild ride.

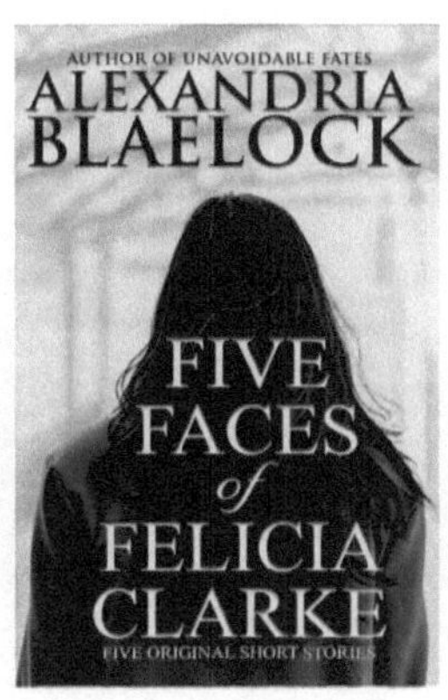

Felicia Clarke; influencer.

Old Fashioned. Fiercely independent.

Encourages others, but treads her own path.

Dead, but fondly remembered.

By some.

ABOUT THE AUTHOR

Australian author Alexandria Blaelock writes mostly fantasy and mystery.

She's appeared in the Stringybark Anthology *Crowd Surfing, Pulphouse Fiction Magazine,* and *Ellery Queen's Mystery Magazine.*

She's also written five self-help books applying business techniques to personal matters like getting dressed, tidying up, and feeding friends.

Discover more at alexandriablaelock.com..

Be the first to know!

Just sign up to receive my Insider Updates so you can stay up to date on my writing, get advance notice of new releases, discounts, free eBooks and much, much more in my monthly communiqués.

At alexandriablaelock.com/insider-updates/

www.ingramcontent.com/pod-product-compliance
Lightning Source LLC
Chambersburg PA
CBHW031254210726
48287CB00003B/1038